The Crowded Hut

retold by Lenika Gael • illustrated by Alexandra Colombo

Visualize

What do you think you would hear if you were in this picture?

zZZZZZ

Once there was a large family that lived in a very tiny hut. The father, Ben, and the mother, Hannah, had seven children. There were three sisters and four brothers.

Ben and Hannah loved their seven children, but they were tired of all the noise and mess. There was always a baby crying, or a sister singing, or a brother acting silly. Seven children make a lot of commotion!

Inside the hut, there was only one small room where the children could play. It was also the room where Ben and Hannah prepared the family's meals. It was very crowded and very loud, all the time.

"These children make too much noise!" said
Ben. "They are always banging and shouting.
There's not enough room for all of us in this
tiny hut. What will we do?"

Hannah was a very wise woman, and she had an idea. "I know just what to do," she said. She went to the market and bought a nice, plump rooster.

She carried the rooster inside her family's tiny hut. The baby cried. He thought maybe it wasn't a good idea to bring a rooster into the hut.

The baby was right! Now the hut was even more crowded. The rooster crowed all day and night. The children couldn't hear each other, so they shouted even louder. Ben was miserable.

But Hannah wasn't finished with her plan. The next day, she bought a round, friendly cow from her friend the farmer. She pushed the cow inside her family's tiny hut.

Now the hut was even more crowded! The cow mooed, the rooster crowed, and the children played. It was so loud that Ben couldn't think. It was so crowded that Ben couldn't move. Ben was miserable.

But Hannah wasn't finished with her plan. The next day, she bought a curious goat from her next-door neighbor. She dragged the goat inside her family's tiny hut.

Now the hut was even more crowded! The goat bleated and chewed on the children's clothes. The cow mooed and bumped into the furniture. The rooster crowed all day and night. Ben was miserable. And now the children were, too!

But Hannah wasn't finished with her plan. She took the goat, the cow, and the rooster out of the tiny hut and put them in the yard. The baby thought this was a very good idea.

"The hut is so quiet and peaceful now!" said Ben. "It doesn't feel crowded at all. I like it!"